For many years a birchbark canoe—etched with the symbol of
an owl on its bow—leaned against the porch at the summer cottage
of the Roosevelt family on Campobello Island, New Brunswick.

What stories could that old canoe hold? Perhaps the first story
began when Franklin Roosevelt, who would become the thirty-
second president of the United States, was only ten years old.

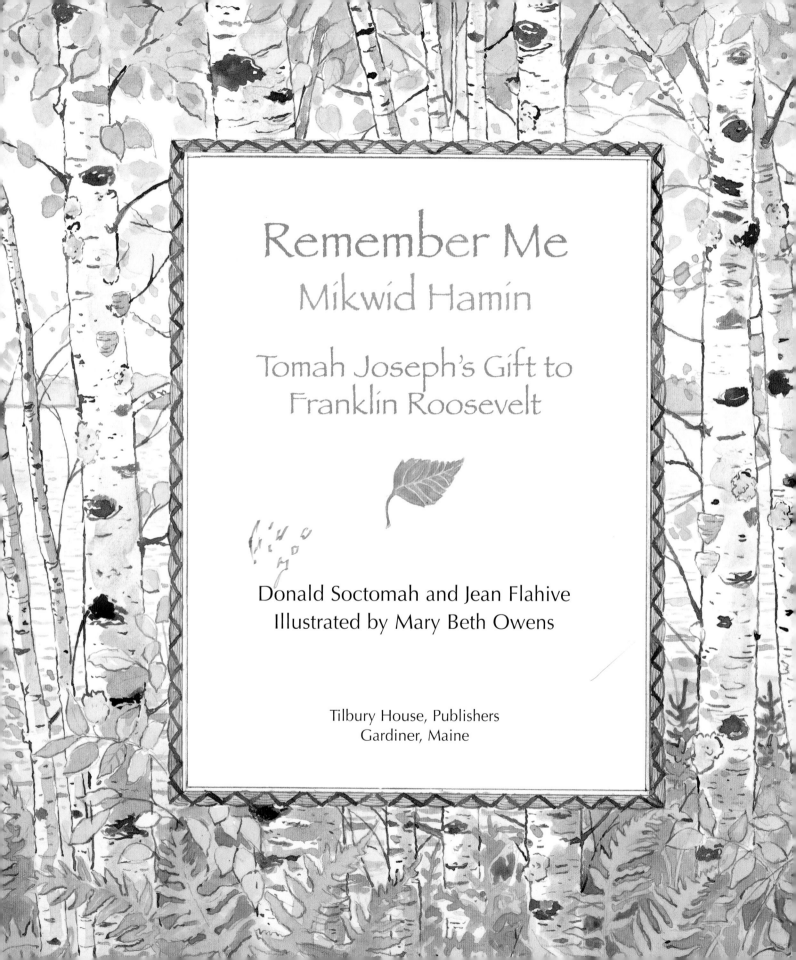

Remember Me
Mikwid Hamin

Tomah Joseph's Gift to Franklin Roosevelt

Donald Soctomah and Jean Flahive
Illustrated by Mary Beth Owens

Tilbury House, Publishers
Gardiner, Maine

Franklin ran down the hillside and onto the beach, his eyes searching the bay. The wet sand cooled his bare feet as the waves splashed over his toes. He smiled to himself and thought, "Today Tomah Joseph will teach me how to paddle a canoe."

Tomah Joseph was once chief of the Passamaquoddy, the tribe that lived on the shores of Passamaquoddy Bay and on the lakes along the St. Croix River.

"For thousands of years the Passamaquoddy knew how to find and make all they needed to live from the land and the sea around them," Franklin's father had told him. "But with the arrival of so many settlers to the area, the Indians' way of life had to change. Now many Indians make their living as fishing and hunting guides. They help summer visitors like us, who come to Campobello Island."

At last the boy spotted Tomah Joseph in the distance. With long, nimble strokes the Indian guide brought the canoe straight to where Franklin stood, slowing just before he reached the beach.

Watching him, Franklin wondered if Tomah Joseph missed his old way of living.

"Hello, Tomah Joseph!" Franklin called out as he splashed through the shallow water.

"*Tan Kahk*," Tomah Joseph replied. "How are you?" The Passamaquoddy elder held his paddle flat on the water to steady the canoe. "Climb in at the bow!"

The air smelled salty and the gentle breeze felt moist on Franklin's face. He'd been in many kinds of boats with his father, but this was his first time in a canoe. He leaned over its edge and peered into the green water, pitching the boat sharply to one side.

"Stay in the center," Tomah Joseph cautioned, quickly leaning the other way to steady the boat. "A canoe is less stable than other boats because it's so narrow. It's built to slice through water like a knife."

Tomah Joseph reached under his seat, pulled out a paddle, and handed it to Franklin. "For now, watch how I paddle."

Fascinated by the smooth, steady slap of the paddle, Franklin watched carefully as Tomah Joseph told him, "The islands protect us from the open sea, but the tides and currents of Passamaquoddy Bay can be strong and dangerous. We'll paddle out with the tide, letting it carry us. When the tide returns to land, we'll travel with it again."

Soon they were out in the bay, and at last Tomah Joseph told the eager Franklin to slip his paddle into the water. Franklin reached forward, plunged his paddle into the dark water, and pulled it back toward his hip. He tried not to splash too much. Paddling was harder than it looked.

While he paddled, Franklin delighted in the many sights and sounds surrounding him. An eagle burst from the clouds and skimmed the water looking for fish. Tomah Joseph pointed to the shore and to the eagle's nest at the top of a tall pine. Suddenly a porpoise broke through the water and surfaced near the canoe.

"Keep your paddle to the other side. Then you won't frighten it," Tomah Joseph said quietly. Soon another porpoise joined the first, blowing water into the air.

Franklin watched the porpoises swim so close he could almost reach out and touch them. Tomah Joseph explained that porpoises are sacred in the Passamaquoddy culture. "They have saved my people from starvation countless times. But we never hunt more than we need."

By late afternoon they turned the canoe with the incoming tide and paddled back to the beach. Tired but excited about his day, Franklin asked, "May I come out with you again?"

"Your father told me I may take you on many paddles," Tomah Joseph replied, pleased that the boy had enjoyed his first lesson.

Franklin paddled often with Tomah Joseph. He learned to handle the canoe when the winds blew strong and the waves pushed their small boat over the rising swells of the sea.

One morning while waiting for the fog to roll out of the bay, Tomah Joseph and Franklin sat on the beach beside the canoe.

"How do you build your canoes?" Franklin asked.

"I make the skin of my canoes from the winter bark of the white birch," Tomah Joseph answered. "In early spring I search the forests for just the right birch. The tree must be tall and straight, and the bark must be thick and healthy."

"Do you have to cut the tree down to peel the bark?"

"No. I start from the bottom of the tree and with my knife peel its bark as I work my way high up the tree. Then I roll it into one long piece. The tree goes on living," Tomah Joseph said. "For the ribs, planks, and paddles I use wood from ash and cedar trees. I use roots from spruce trees to bind it all together. Last, I use spruce gum and a mixture of animal fat to seal the seams so it is watertight."

Franklin looked thoughtfully at his guide. The Passamaquoddy elder was teaching him so much more than just how to paddle a canoe.

In late July, Franklin helped Tomah Joseph gather sweetgrass, the fragrant blades of tall, thin grass that grew in the marshes along the shore. Tomah Joseph showed Franklin how to pinch the grass blade by blade as a way to honor the spirit in each leaf of the sacred plant. Like many of his people, Tomah Joseph believed that sweetgrass was the first plant to cover the earth.

When Tomah Joseph made baskets out of birchbark, he often added a coil of sweetgrass to the rim. He etched the birchbark with pictures of animals and people, and then framed the scenes with geometric designs. When he was finished, Tomah Joseph signed his work by etching his name on the basket.

Franklin had seen Tomah Joseph's baskets in the homes of Campobello summer residents. He thought the baskets were beautiful but he puzzled over what the pictures meant.

"When I work with birchbark," Tomah Joseph told Franklin as they collected sweetgrass, "I remember the Old Time. I remember my ancestors and their stories, and I feel happy then."

"Is that what the pictures are—stories?" Franklin asked.

Tomah Joseph smiled. "Yes, each picture tells a story of the Old Time."

"Will you tell me one of these stories?"

For a moment Tomah Joseph was quiet, and then he began to speak.

"A long time ago, a young boy was lost in the woods. He was very cold and scared. When night came he sought shelter from the bitter wind and went into a cave. Big Mother Bear was in the cave with her cubs, but she did not hurt the boy. Instead, she nestled him with her cubs to keep him warm. In the days that followed, the bears and the boy gathered berries for food and the boy lived with Mother Bear and her cubs through the long winter. In time, my people found the boy. They would not kill the bear because while the boy was lost she had become his mother. In this way they honored her. And that is why the boy's descendants became known as the people of the Bear Clan."

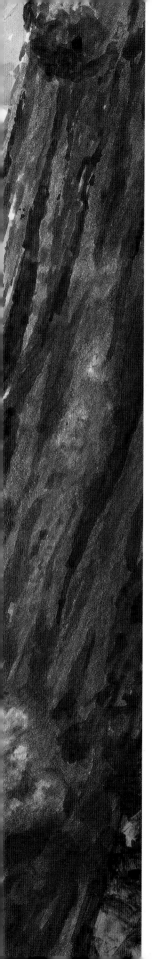

"Do all your people have clans?"

"Yes, every Passamaquoddy family has a special clan: the Eagle, the Raven, the Frog, the Wolf, and many others. The people of the Eagle Clan will always protect the eagle."

"And the eagle will protect them?" Franklin asked.

Tomah Joseph nodded. He looked gently at the boy who had spent so many afternoons with him. "There is another thing about the animals, Franklin. Indians believe that within each person is the spirit of an animal. This animal is their spirit helper."

"A spirit helper?"

Speaking in a near whisper, Tomah Joseph turned to Franklin and said, "*Ko-ko-gus*, the owl, is my spirit helper."

"He is?" Franklin whispered back.

"Yes, many times as a young boy I noticed an owl was always nearby to alert me in times of danger. I asked my grandmother why this was so. She told me that the Ancient Ones believed the great Creator told the owl that if people listen to his voice, they will know what is to come. And so I listen."

Together they started out across the blueberry barrens.

Franklin could barely contain himself. He blurted out, "Do I have one, too? Tell me, please! What animal is mine?"

Tomah Joseph laughed. "Patience, Franklin. When you are alone with nature, in the forest or on the water, and your heart is quiet, you will find your spirit helper."

Like other wealthy families of the time, the Roosevelts often traveled to Europe in summer, but Franklin was always happiest when his family returned to their cottage on Campobello Island. Here he was free to explore the beauty and wonder of this special place.

In the fall Franklin would return to his family's home in Hyde Park, New York. Then Tomah Joseph would travel to his people's winter home many miles inland from Campobello to Peter Dana Point in Maine. "When the grasses die," he said to Franklin, pointing to the brown fields, "I leave, too."

Years later in early summer, twenty-three-year-old Franklin spotted Tomah Joseph paddling his canoe to shore. As was his custom for so many years, Franklin hurried to the beach to greet him.

"It's good to see you," Franklin said with a wide smile.

"*Tan Kahk*," Tomah Joseph replied. His hair was white as snow.

"What a beautiful new canoe!"

Tomah Joseph handed the paddle to Franklin.

"I am growing old, and you, my friend, are growing into a fine young man who has many important journeys ahead. Since you were a boy, you have walked in friendship with me. This canoe is my gift to you."

"*Woliwon*, Tomah Joseph. Thank you." Franklin held the paddle tight. "I have learned so many things from you. *Woliwon*."

Franklin ran his hand over the canoe and spotted an owl etched in the bow. "*Ko-ko-gus!* Your spirit helper." He smiled at Tomah Joseph. "Now I know you will share in my journeys."

The Indian elder gently touched Franklin's hand. "You are like *Ko-ko-gus*. One day people will listen to your voice."

For the rest of the summer, Franklin paddled his canoe, tucking in and out of craggy coves and sharing the sea with eagles, ospreys, terns, and gulls. He even spotted a pod of whales swimming beyond the fish weirs that hugged the island.

Later that summer, when the air was crisp and the grasses faded to brown, Tomah Joseph appeared unexpectedly at the Roosevelt cottage.

Franklin welcomed him and asked, "Are you leaving the island for your winter home? Will I see you next summer?"

Tomah Joseph did not answer. Instead he cast a long gaze at the fiery sunset across the bay. A flock of geese flew by. Finally he spoke. "I am like the geese. Soon I will go to another place in the sky. *Mikwid hamin*, Franklin. Always remember me."

Saying no more, Tomah Joseph walked slowly away, following the worn footpath that led from the Roosevelt cottage into the forest.

Franklin Roosevelt (1882–1945) became the thirty-second president
of the United States. He loved spending time in the summers on
Campobello, which he referred to as his "beloved island."

The canoe that Tomah Joseph built for Franklin Roosevelt
is on display in the Visitor Center at the Roosevelt Campobello
International Park. If you look carefully, you will see
the owl motif etched on the canoe.

GOV TOMAH JOSEPH
PASSAMAQUODDY TRIbE

Tomah Joseph (1837–1914) distinguished himself as a gifted artist
by etching scenes from his people's origin stories onto
his birchbark creations. He often added the words *Mikwid hamin*—
remember me—to these scenes.

TILBURY HOUSE, PUBLISHERS   103 Brunswick Avenue, Gardiner, ME 04345   800-582-1899   www.tilburyhouse.com

First hardcover edition: June 2009 • 10 9 8 7 6 5 4 3 2 1

DEDICATIONS

Tomah Joseph was a very special man with unique art skills that have ancient traditional meanings, an art form that is carried on by his descendants in the Passamaquoddy Tribe. So I dedicate this book to Tomah Joseph and his present and future descendants, which include three of my daughters and their children. They will be the ones who will keep his memory alive. "Long Live the Spirit of Tomah Joseph!" —DS

To FDR and Tomah Joseph, who now belong to the Old Time. —JF

Library of Congress Cataloging-in-Publication Data
Soctomah, Donald.
Remember me, mikwid hamin : Tomah Joseph's gift to Franklin Roosevelt / Donald Soctomah and Jean Flahive ; illustrated by Mary Beth Owens. —1st hardcover ed.
    p. cm.
Summary: Spending his childhood summers on Campobello Island, young Franklin Delano Roosevelt learns how to canoe and something about the Passamaquoddy culture from Tomah Joseph, a respected fishing and canoe guide, basketmaker and canoe-builder, and former chief of his tribe.
ISBN 978-0-88448-300-7 (hardcover : alk. paper)
1. Roosevelt, Franklin D. (Franklin Delano), 1882-1945—Childhood and youth—Juvenile fiction. 2. Joseph, Tomah, 1837-1914—Juvenile fiction. [1. Roosevelt, Franklin D. (Franklin Delano), 1882-1945—Childhood and youth—Fiction. 2. Joseph, Tomah, 1837-1914—Fiction. 3. Passamaquoddy Indians—Fiction. 4. Indians of North America—Maine—Fiction. 5. Canoes and canoeing—Fiction. 6. Campobello Island (N.B.)—History—19th century—Fiction. 7. Canada—History—1867-1914—Fiction.] I. Flahive, Jean. II. Owens, Mary Beth, ill. III. Title.
    PZ7.S685254Re 2009
    [E]—dc22   2008045961

Designed by Geraldine Millham, Westport, Massachusetts
Printed and bound by Sung In Printing, South Korea